For Longiswa, my Kwela Jamela

What's Cooking, Jamela? copyright © Frances Lincoln Limited 2001

Text and illustrations copyright © Niki Daly 2001

By arrangement with The Inkman, Cape Town, South Africa

Hand-lettering by Andrew van der Merwe

First published in Great Britain in 2001 by Frances Lincoln Children's Books,
4 Torriano Mews, Torriano Avenue, London NW5 2RZ
www.franceslincoln.com

First paperback edition 2002

British Library Cataloguing in Publication Data available on request

ISBN 978-0-7112-1705-8

Set in Bembo

Printed in Singapore

5 7 9 8 6

What's Cooking, Jamela?

STORY + PICTURES by Niki DALY

F

FRANCES LINCOLN
CHILDREN'S BOOKS

Gogo and Mama were making plans for Christmas.

"I'll make the pudding. You can do a chicken," said Gogo.

"And Thelma will cook a nice rice and *marogo* stew," said Mama.

"Good," said Gogo. "We'll have a lovely Christmas meal."

Jamela knew all about Christmas. It was a time to celebrate baby Jesus' birthday with a nativity play at school. Christmas also meant Christmas presents and getting together with the family.

When Gogo left, Mama said, "Come Jamela, let's go to Mrs Zibi and buy one of her young chickens. If we feed it well, it will be nice and fat for Christmas."

Mama let Jamela choose the chicken – a nice red one. Mrs Zibi gave them a bag of *mielies*.

"We can call her Christmas," said Jamela. Mama laughed. "That's a good name for a Christmas chicken, Jamela."

When they got home, Mama showed Jamela how much water and mielies the chicken would need every day.

"See if she will eat out of your hand," suggested Mama. Nervously, Jamela held out a handful of yellow mielies.

"Look, Mama, she's eating!" squealed Jamela.

"Now it's time to feed my own chick," said Mama, smiling.

Before she went to bed, Jamela asked, "How long until Christmas, Mama?"

"When our chicken is nice and fat, then it will be Christmas," replied Mama.

Every morning before school, Jamela gave Christmas food and water. If there was time, she let Christmas sit on her lap and hand-fed her mielies.

That bird just loved to eat! Mama scooped up the chicken droppings, which she used to make fertilizer to feed her marrows. Every day the chicken and the marrows seemed to grow rounder and larger.

Whenever Gogo visited, she asked, "How is our Christmas meal doing?" Jamela frowned and said, "She's doing fine, Gogo." But she didn't like the way Gogo licked her lips – like the lady on the fried chicken TV commercial.

At school, they did a nativity play. There were angels and African dancers. Jamela played Mary, and carried baby Jesus on her back like a real mama. Vuyo was a very handsome Joseph in his Basutu hat and blanket.

Tabu, Elliot and Zingi were splendid wise men in their Madiba shirts.

They sang "Away in a Manger" and other Christmas songs to the sound of *marimbas* and drums. Everyone clapped and sang along.

When Jamela and Mama got home, Jamela made a manger for Christmas.

"That's a lovely manger, but I hope you're not growing too fond of that chicken," said Mama.

"No, Mama," sang Jamela, as she ran outside calling, "Christmas! Chick, chick – come and see what I've made for you!"

Mama was worried when she saw how happy Jamela and the big fat chicken looked, sitting side by side. Just how would she get the chicken away from Jamela and into a pot?

The day before Christmas, Mrs Zibi came round.

"Jamela, please go and see how Thelma is getting on with the rice and marogo," said Mama.

Jamela looked at Mrs Zibi's big hands as they rubbed against her apron. They looked ready for serious business.

"Stop staring and go now, Jamela," said Mama.

Jamela knew it was bad manners to argue with grown-ups,
but she didn't like the look of things.

"OK, Mama," said Jamela, as she set off to Thelma's house …

… with Christmas in her arms.

Christmas flapped and squawked. She almost flew out of Jamela's arms.

"Do you want to sell that chicken?" called a lady who was cooking chicken legs for her customers.

Jamela shook her head – "*Aikona*!" – and hurried along.

"Toot! toot!" a taxi hooted. Startled, Jamela jumped, and let go of Christmas. Laughter filled the taxi rank as the chicken scrambled between legs and disappeared into the crowd.

"Christmas, chick chick!" wailed Jamela. But Christmas was nowhere to be seen. Gone!

Jamela walked slowly home. At the end of her road, she saw
Mama and Mrs Zibi running towards her. Mama looked worried.
Mrs Zibi looked cross. How Jamela wished she could grow wings
and fly over their heads, down the road and far, far away.

"Where's the chicken?" panted Mrs Zibi.

Jamela flapped her arms weakly. "Gone," she said.

"Oh, Jamela!" sighed Mama.

Jamela looked sorry – but inside she was smiling. Wherever Christmas was, she was not in anyone's pot!

Mama took Jamela firmly by the hand and they walked home. When they passed Archie, Mama greeted him, "*Molo*, Archie. Have you seen our chicken?"

"Aikona," replied Archie. "But if I do, I'll tell it that you ladies are looking for it."

Down the road, Old Greasy Hands was revving up a car.

"Molo, Greasy Hands!" shouted Mama over the noise.

"Have you seen our chicken?"

"Whaaat?" shouted Greasy Hands.

Just then, a taxi skidded to a stop.

The passengers shouted, "*Hamba*! Get it out, get it out!"
The taxi door opened and out jumped a plump red chicken.
    Christmas fluffed out her feathers, then took off – over the
pavement and into Miss Style's hairdressing salon.
    "Quick, quick!" shouted Mama.

Inside the salon, Christmas was running wild over counters
and half-braided ladies. Hairdryers, shampoo, combs, braids
and beads went flying.

Mama grabbed a basket and cornered Christmas.

"VIVA!" shouted the ladies,
when Mama managed to throw
a basket over the frantic chicken.

Mrs Zibi thrust her hands under the basket and pulled out Christmas. "From the basket to the pot!" she hollered.

"Oh Mama, Mama! Please don't let Mrs Zibi hurt Christmas!" cried Jamela.

"A chicken is a chicken!" snapped Mrs Zibi.

"Christmas is not a chicken," cried Jamela. "Christmas is my friend. And you can't eat friends."

Mama looked at the ladies for help. But the ladies were all smiling sweetly at Jamela.

"You can't eat friends," echoed the ladies.

"*Ga*, nonsense!" scolded Mrs Zibi.

On Christmas morning, Jamela helped Mama prepare their Christmas meal. The rich chicken fertilizer had given the marrows soft, succulent flesh. Jamela scooped out the pips and put them aside. Mama filled the hollow with a mixture of nuts, breadcrumbs, butter and tasty herbs.

By the time Gogo and the other family members arrived, mouth-watering smells filled the kitchen.

Gogo sniffed and asked, "What's cooking, Jamela?"

"It's a surprise, Gogo," Jamela replied.

After everyone had exchanged presents, Mama invited the family to the table and served the food. Steam danced around Thelma's rice and marogo stew. Mama took the lid off the delicious-smelling baked marrow.

Jamela could see Gogo's eyes searching for the chicken. But Gogo didn't say anything. Everyone was happy to be enjoying a Christmas Day meal together.

After the pudding, Gogo rubbed her tummy. Then, looking at Mama, she said. "*Haai*! That was better than a five-star hotel. But, *Sisi*, where is the chicken?"

Jamela jumped up from the table.

"I'll show you, Gogo," she said. Grabbing Gogo's hand, she led her out into the yard, where Christmas was enjoying a tasty feast of marrow pips.

"Look, Gogo – there's the chicken!" said Jamela. "Mama has given her to me for a Christmas present. Her name is Christmas."

Gogo looked at the beautiful chicken, but she didn't lick her lips. Instead, she hugged Jamela against her full tummy and said, "Well, it looks like a very happy Christmas to me."

You bet!

GLOSSARY

Aikona (Xhosa/Zulu): No!

Ga (Afrikaans): an exclamation of disgust

Haai (Xhosa): an exclamation of surprise

Hamba (Nguni): Go away!

Marimbas (possibly Swahili): African xylophone

Marogo (Sotho): green vegetable leaves used for cooking

Mielies (Afrikaans): corn

Molo (Xhosa): hello

Sisi (Xhosa): sister. African woman are addressed as "sisi",
(except older women who are called "mama").
A mother calls her daughter "sisi" as an endearment.

Viva: Portugese victory salute found in Angolo and
Mozambique, now used as a cry of celebration.

MORE JAMELA STORIES BY NIKI DALY
FROM FRANCES LINCOLN CHILDREN'S BOOKS

Happy Birthday Jamela

It's nearly Jamela's birthday, and she longs for the sparkly
Princess Shoes she's seen in the shoe shop to go with her party dress.
But Mama says no, Jamela's new shoes will have to be worn for school too.
Back in her room, Jamela sadly unwraps the strong black school shoes
Mama has bought her – and suddenly she has a brilliant idea…

Jamela's Dress

Mama is very pleased with the dress material she has bought
for Thelma's wedding. Jamela can't resist wrapping the material around her,
and before she knows it, she is sashaying down the road to show
Thelma her beautiful dress! When things go wrong, Mama is sad indeed,
but there's a happy ending just in time for Thelma's wedding day.

Where's Jamela?

There's no place like home. So when Jamela is faced with moving
to a new house with Mama and Gogo, she decides that she wants
to stay right where she is. But when the trunk is packed
and ready to go, where is Jamela?

A delightful story in which Jamela discovers that
home is where the heart is.

Frances Lincoln titles are available from all good bookshops.
You can also buy books and find out more about your favourite titles,
authors and illustrators on our website: www.franceslincoln.com